The
Valentine Sheep

Story by:
William Rogers Boone

Words by:
Bonnie Boone Jennings

Illustrations by:
Becky Boone Keck

This Book Belongs to:

_____

AuthorHouse™
1663 Liberty Drive
Bloomington, IN 47403
www.authorhouse.com
Phone: 833-262-8899

Because of the dynamic nature of the Internet, any web addresses or links contained in this book may have changed
since publication and may no longer be valid. The views expressed in this work are solely those of the author and do not
necessarily reflect the views of the publisher, and the publisher hereby disclaims any responsibility for them.

This book is printed on acid-free paper.

ISBN: 978-1-4259-9046-6 (sc)

Library of Congress Control Number: 2007900391

Print information available on the last page.

Published by AuthorHouse 03/31/2022

authorHOUSE®

This book is dedicated to:

Danielle

Stephen

Caitlyn

Natalie

Zach

Once there was a lamb named Felicity,

who was having breakfast with her family.

It was February, and the grass was rather bare,

so she decided to search for food elsewhere.

She wandered to the edge of the wood,

and watched a squirrel playing as she stood.

Sally Squirrel was searching for acorns to find,

and Felicity followed, leaving her cares behind.

Felicity and Sally had a contest.

Finding the most acorns was the quest.

The two raced here to there.

The lamb and squirrel made a funny pair.

Sally Squirrel was as quick as could be,

Running and leaping from tree to tree.

The adventure led them into the forest deep.

And Felicity couldn't hear her mother's plea.

Felicity grew tired of the squirrel's chase

and wanted to explore at a slower pace.

She noticed Tom Turtle creeping along,

and asked if he minded if she tagged along.

Tom was headed for the river to sun.

Felicity thought it sounded like fun.

On the way to the river there was so much to see,

and Felicity loved being this carefree.

She had never seen the river before.

It was such an exciting place to explore.

There were new smells to smell and new

animals to meet.

This whole adventure sure was neat.

At the edge of the river, stood Ollie Otter.
Ollie was playing with his family in the water.

Felicity stopped to have a drink.

Seeing the otter family made her think,

Of the games she played with her sister and brother.

She began to miss them, and her father and mother.

Where she was now, Felicity wasn't quite sure.

There wasn't a sign of her little pasture.

Felicity was lost and she began to cry.

Finding her family would be hard, but she had to try.

She realized how worried they all must be.

She was lucky to have such a family.

As it turns out, it was Valentine's Day.

And Felicity saw Cupid, while on her way.

He stopped when he heard the little lamb's plea,

And agreed to help her find her family.

From Cupid's view up in the sky,

He could see Felicity's pasture nearby.

Using his arrows and his bow,

He shot down hearts for Felicity to follow.

Felicity followed the hearts as they fell,

Knowing that soon all would be well.

The hearts led her past the river and wood,

Until she saw the field where her family stood.

They had been searching for her all about

And when they saw her, they began to shout.

Felicity told them how she made it home,

And promised from now on not to roam.

Cupid then gave the lambs a special treat,

It was a heart shaped cookie for them all to eat.

They realized the importance of each loved one.

And that is how a tradition was begun.

Each year to celebrate this special date,

The lambs make heart cookies to decorate.

You and Your family can celebrate too,

With the cookie recipe we've included for you.

You can make these cookies to share or keep

And remember the story of the Valentine Sheep.

Felicity's Sugar Cookie Recipe

Ingredients:
1 cup butter
1 cup granulated sugar
2 eggs
1 tsp vanilla
½ tsp lemon flavoring
2 cups flour
1 tsp baking powder
Pinch of salt

Directions:

1. In small bowl, mix flour, baking powder and salt. Set aside.
2. In large bowl, cream butter and sugar until smooth.
3. Beat in eggs, one at a time.
4. Add the vanilla and lemon flavorings.
5. Gradually add flour mixture, about ½ cup at a time.
6. Cover dough and chill for 1 to 2 hours.
7. Preheat oven to 400 degrees. Lightly grease cookie sheets.
8. On a lightly floured board, roll out dough to about ¼ inch thick.
9. Cut into heart shapes. Sprinkle with sugar (or frost cookie after cooling).
10. Bake for 6 to 8 minutes until light brown on the edges.

About the Authors

William R. "Bill" Boone always had a love for animals. He became particulary fond of sheep while working on a sheep farm during high school. Bill continued to work with sheep while in college and used them as a focus for his graduate studies. Today, Bill is a lab director at the Greenville Hospital System in Greenville, SC. He resides in Simpsonville, SC with his wife, Edna, and enjoys spending time with his five grandchildren.

Bonnie Boone Jennings grew up with a love for animals and was always trying to care for the injured. Once as a child, Bonnie brought home a lamb with a broken leg and kept it in the garage until it was strong enough to go back to the farm. Upon completeing her MBA degree, Bonnie moved to Mt. Pleasant, SC with her husband, Blair. She enjoys spending time with their three children, Caitlyn, Natalie and Zachary. Bonnie volunteers at her childrens' school and her church.

Becky Boone Keck was always drawing and making crafts as a child. While living in Keota, IA, her parents enrolled her in an art course. Here she learned the joy of painting. Today, Becky resides in Myrtle Beach, SC with her husband, Eric, and their two children, Danielle and Stephen. Becky is a Professor of Anatomy and Physiology at Horry Georgetown Technical College in Conway, SC. She enjoys painting and working with children. Becky volunteers with the local elementary school.

Origin of the Story

On Valentine's Day each year, young Bill would wake up to find two large heart-shaped sugar cookies on the kitchen table, one for him and one for his brother, Mike. The cookies were elegantly decorated by his mother as a special Valentine's treat. When Bill had children, he continued the family tradition and baked one heart shaped cookie for each of his four children. One day, one of his children asked, "Who made the cookies?" Bill thought for a moment, 'Easter has Peter Rabbit, Christmas has Santa Claus and Rudolph the Red-Nose Reindeer, Thanksgiving has a Turkey so why not an animal for Valentine's Day. Having a love for sheep, Bill replied, "The Valentine Sheep brought you those cookies while you were sleeping." And so, the Valentine Sheep was born. The story of the Valentine Sheep came to be when Bonnie took her father's idea and made it into a poem. She named the lamb Felicity from the Spanish work Feliz meaning "happy." Becky read the story and drew the pictures, bringing Felicity to life. The girls presented their father with the book one Christmas as a symbol of family love and togetherness.

Printed in the United States
by Baker & Taylor Publisher Services